Refusing to Grow 4

The Real Estate Tycoon that bulldozed his way
to the top.

A. Ruben

Printed in the United States of America.

Refusing to Grow 4: The Real Estate Tycoon that bulldozed his way to the top / Ruben

ISBN: 978-0-9754590-7-2

Ickynicks Publishing

Front Cover by Adam Zillins

The following story is based upon actual events and people. However the timeline of events has been compressed and edited to accommodate the story and its characters. Any similarity of dramatized characters, incidents, companies, or attributes to any actual person, living or dead, or to any actual event or to any existing organization is entirely coincidental and unintentional.

Note to the Reader

The following chronological series of semi-disconnected incidents are based on true events and characters, which capture certain personalities perhaps too ridiculous to imagine. Yet, they are neither exaggerations nor embellishments.

Preface

While Arthur was adding $7 million to a company in Los Angeles and then later surpassing his quota in Cleveland, his sister, Shannon, was in the midst of her own mind-boggling misadventures.

At first she thought her brother was just exaggerating when he shared his stories of the ineptitude he was dealing with, but then Shannon got to experience her own. From one paradigm of pinball lunacy to another she couldn't believe it how absurd some people and businesses were, prompting her to think about opening up her own.

While her brother dealt with a runaway locomotive hypomanic son and heir to the company in LA, she was faced with staggering ineptitude. While he was dealing with a sexist vice-president she had a boss who publicly derided his employees, calling them spoiled rotten.

From a daycare eclipsed by a class action lawsuit to an unethical superintendent of schools to later to a real estate company beset by incompetent management, she began to realize that what holds success back isn't profit or processes, but people!

While Arthur faced weak owner-parents in LA, Shannon experienced a whirlwind of ineptitude and blatant disregard for common sense, from banshee-bosses shouting at co-workers to frivolous spending in recessed economies. It seemed there was a madhouse of idiocy around her.

Brought up like her brother, Shannon was raised with a strong work ethic and moral principles, such as helping others, but as the economy tanked she too had to find work wherever she could. Unfortunately, this meant discovering just how many incompetent bosses were on the crusade to eradicate logic and reason. This is her story.

Cast of Characters:

Shannon – a young college graduate, who will apply her talents of social marketing to earn a job in a down market.

Tobias – a real estate broker and owner, who will fire his employees as often as he checks himself in the mirror.

Roxanne / Roxy – Tobias' wife, her short temper, excessive jewelry and demand for complete subservience from her employees will go so far as to remove the break room so her employees can't take a lunch.

Victoria – an educational superintendent whose strong-armed leadership will hinder an already burdened school system. Her unscrupulous actions will launch an auditing investigation, revealing secrets of unethical behavior.

Robby – the Head of Human Resources, who will succumb to Victoria's pressure and resign, only to be later vindicated.

Acknowledgements

The author wishes to thank the following for their support, Lynn, Marilyn, Alex, Sara, Rochelle and Mike. Thank you very much for your assistance in making this work possible.

The following is based on a true story.

Chapters

The Leadership

Chapter 1

The Real Estate Tycoon

At 7 AM sharp, Tobias drove up to the office pleased to see his employees already at work. Good. That's the way it should be. His name was clearly spelled out on his license plate so that everyone knew it was him, and on his second car was the company's website. His wife, Roxy, had her name on her plate along with #1. And why not, they were #1 after all.

In an area where most agents averaged .89% of their real estate market, he owned 2.54%, owing largely to his focus on low priced homes, which was less than $100,000. On average, his bread and butter were homes in the range of $50-65,000. In a business quarter, he averaged about $57,000; he listed and sold nearly double his competition.

Having only been in business just a few years, Tobias had pushed his way to the top by selling in volume. Unlike his competition that wet their lips on homes over $200,000, he went after smaller bricks, pocketing a little bit each time, but allowing it to add up over time.

Nearly every morning he drove to work listening to his business coach's recordings, knowing that he was the best, because the CD said so. After all, his next closest competitor only owned 1.4% and sold half as many; his office shelf proudly displayed his diamond awards.

He had six business coaches and had written on his conference board in big, bold letters, WAYS TO GROW! He never erased it nor did he ever use the board for any other purpose. What for? Those words said it all... and the fact that he sat right in front of it underscored the point. Whatever ways to grow there were came from Tobias and him alone.

He discarded naysayers, typically terminating at least one employee a month, if nothing else to keep everyone on their toes. "My shit accomplishes more than you do," he once said to an agent he fired. In an eleventh-month period he fired four agents, two office assistants, and his social media-marketing specialist; four others quit before they were fired.

Of his average six agents, his top two closed 93 homes between them. Both had been employed the longest at three years, having figured out Tobias. The rest came and went, averaging no more than a year and a half. But despite two top agents, Tobias still referred to them as "spoiled rotten," which he had no problem stating on his reports.

And whereas other offices gave their agents higher commissions, sometimes as high as 70% to encourage more sales, he only gave 20% to his, and why not? After all, he had nothing but a bunch of crybabies, as he liked to say, which he unreservedly posted on social media, particularly when posting new jobs: "Looking for people with great social skills as are office is growing... we have been number 1 in total market share for years because we don't hire cry babies. If you want to grow in all ways in your life then this is the office with only winners in the room."

He fired as often as he hired. "Shit or be shitted on the pot," he liked to say, either putting his own twist on the phrase or not realizing it was actually, "shit or get off the pot." But with so many agents coming and going, and all 10-99 employees, he not only treated them like they were second-class citizens, but also frankly didn't care.

He was #1 of 900 agents, #1 the last five years, and #1 in market share, and so he frankly didn't care what anyone had to say. When he fired an agent's wife, who was an office assistant, the agent stormed into his office, demanding an explanation.

"She's been working for you for four years and you inexplicably decide one day just to fire her? You have like six business coaches. Fire one of them! And on top of that, you want all of us to pay to go to seminars on how to build teams. And yet, you're firing people like my wife and four others! How is that building any sort of team?"

"You can say whatever you want and learn from it," Tobias said, indifferently.

"I see. So this is just business to you. It isn't about helping others or about caring about people or their livelihoods. You give people no warnings. You just fire them whenever you feel like it. Is that it?" He tried to restrain his temper, but Tobias's response could not be weathered.

"Of course. I'm the boss. You don't like it go work somewhere else. I don't need you here. I don't need crybabies like you! Go cry on somebody else's shoulder."

"I was in education administration for over twenty-five years. What you're doing is not building teams! You have to give somebody a warning first. That's the right thing to do."

"Oh boo-hoo. My wife got fired and I'm all upset," he said mockingly. "If you're done crying then go out and get me sales. Otherwise, shit or get shitted on the pot."

"It's shit or get off the pot!"

"I'll say it however I want! Now get your ass out of my office and sell some goddamn houses!" Tobias then turned to everyone in the office. "And that goes to the rest of you. Do your job and sell. You're all a waste of human space, every last one of you. Hamsters fucking accomplish more than you people do!"

Chapter 2

Way Too Much Jewelry

Roxy came to the office like a feudal landowner coming to inspect the peasantry. As soon as she stepped in she started correcting people. "Why aren't you smiling? Oh not that much. Turn that face away from me." Bracelets hid half her arm and rings veiled her fingers. She wore gold in her ears and everywhere else. She loved gold. She loved its color, its glisten, and the fact that she could display more of it than anyone else pleased her immensely.

"Good morning my employees," she said every day, strutting over to them as if interested, but really wanting to just see them hard at work. "Are you happy today?" she asked. Employees who had been there long enough had learned to just say, "yes ma'am. Thank you."

There was nothing that excited her more than happy employees hard at work as well as lovely remarks about her jewelry. "Oh thank you," she once replied to someone trying to be flattering. "I wish I could say the same to you."

As she entered her office every morning, she turned to and wished everyone a good day, which would have been perfectly fine if it wasn't followed by her remark, "I wish I didn't have to pay all of you, but I do."

Not just snooty but hypocritical also, she forbid others from listening to music while at their desk. This was not only put into policy, but then she blatantly disobeyed it by turning up her own music so everyone could hear. "You need to work. I'm just here to supervise."

She belittled employees as she distrusted them, going so far as to count every envelope and stamp and then, without any evidence, would accuse someone of stealing; she never apologized, even if she threatened to call the police. "You're only here to work, not speak or think."

She fired office assistants like it was a trend going out of style, but really it was because she was bored. She hired and fired as much as Tobias and occasionally acted in her role as a buyer's agent, meaning she helped clients find homes and earned the usual 3% if she closed. But most of the time she preferred to micromanage and make changes to the office.

One particular change she made was removing the office break room. Either she didn't understand that people can get hungry or she simply refused to accept the legality of it, but after having turned it into a storage room she still couldn't understand why employees were taking a lunch.

"Wait, what? Is this the new trend? So now *everyone* is taking a lunch break?" she said, coming around to desks at noon and finding nobody working.

Roxy loved vacationing. She absolutely loved it, but wherever she went it was always to a resort. She didn't care if it was the Caribbean, the tropics, or the dry deserts. She only stayed in high-end resorts that pampered her. She treated herself to spas, massages, and meditation, allowing herself to become liberated from any stress. "This is what I needed," she would say, slipping into bliss.

But she absolutely, without a shadow of a doubt, resented others taking time off. "Aren't you happy working here? Why do you need to take time off when you enjoy what you're doing?" Of course her reasons for vacationing were exempt from such inquires, because she was after all an owner and thus entitled to "retreats."

"I don't take vacations," she told one employee who challenged her frequent time off. "I restore myself to be able to manage you better." Not only was that employee fired, but also Roxy felt so emotionally distraught over it that she took another vacation.

Chapter 3

The Superintendent

Elsewhere, in the public sector, it was 6:08 AM and Victoria hit send on her email sending yet another message to her overwhelmed head of Human Resources, Robby. She had recently been hired in as superintendent with the highest of expectations. The county was in a financial crisis and they had high hopes with hiring her.

She had been a former business manager as well as superintendent in another county, so she clearly had experience in fiscal management. The Board expressed their congratulations to her as they welcomed her aboard and hoped she could help navigate the districts into sounder waters. Aside from its schools, the county also had a career and technical program, services for the deaf & blind as well as special education. But there was simply too much that needed funding and not enough money. Everyone hoped Victoria would be the one to turn things around.

With nearly 13,000 students in the county and a budget of just over $30.6 million the needs were as high as they were constantly evolving. Allocated three ways, the majority of the budget, almost two-thirds of it, went to special education ($19.5 million). The remaining was split between a general fund and the career & technical programs (the former receiving about $6.7 million while the latter only about $4.3 million.) What this really meant was that special education received funding first and foremost before any other fund.

But costs were only rising. The county's technology was in desperate need of updates for example, but every penny was already being spent every month: $2,500 for Internet, $29,000 for wide area network, $31,250 for tech support as well as additional annual expenses including $20,000 for contacted services, $100,000 for hardware updates and $25,000 for network hardware. The only thing manageable was the monthly phone bill at $1,200.

If that wasn't bad already, the price tag for the county's digital technology marketing was an exorbitant $188,000. Compared sharply to the cost of the contract-bid lawn care and yard work, $106,000, that covered 9 districts and all the buildings included and it was no wonder the county was bleeding.

Added to those expenditures was personal. The county staffed 130 employees, including clerical, instructional teachers, custodians and consultants. Of just the instructional staff, the county paid nearly $153,000 a month to them. This was for 22 teachers and 20 paraprofessionals.

But where the bleeding was gushing was special education. Despite receiving two-thirds of the budget it held a deficit of $274,000. The school psychologist and support staff alone cost the county roughly $461,000 a year; the dean transportation system cost over $3.5 million; the assistant superintendent of special ed. had a salary of $98,000, but received the second highest supplemental compensation at just over $10,000.

Supplemental compensation typically includes bonuses, retirement matching programs, or payment for unused vacation days. Compared to the Early Intervention Supervisor, who earned $83,193 but received the single highest supplemental compensation of anyone at roughly $15,500 and thus earning about as much as the assistant superintendent of special ed. Both of these two positions, however, had the highest rate of reimbursed expenses, of just over $9,000 between them, which could be justified from national conferences attended. On the other hand, sometimes they couldn't, like in Victoria's case.

But as the economic situation further declined the Board of Education prayed that Victoria would rescue them. At a starting salary of roughly $148,000, she immediately went to work berating employees and their excuses as lazy. She demanded without reprieve, offered little in the way of praise, and flattered no one but the Board.

She cracked the whip as often as she inundated her staff to sharp criticism. Despite multiple grievances sent to the Board, they were all dismissed; as long as she got results they simply didn't care how she led, even if it was totalitarian.

And so the brunt fell on Robby and the assistant superintendent. Every bit of responsibility was shifted onto them and failure- though not an option- was typically the result. The latter soon resigned under stress, and Robby had to pick up the slack; every missed deadline was another verbal lashing.

"How do you consider yourself a qualified manager?" she said, publicly shaming him. "You're as incompetent as it gets. Anyone could do your job better than you!" She belittled him as often as she scolded, but that didn't ease the flow of responsibilities. While she delegated, he collapsed under its weight: double the emails, double the workload, and staying late until seven or eight o'clock was now standard.

Deadlines were as impractical as they were asinine. How on earth was anyone supposed to post a job position in a day? It's seemed more than reasonable except that this was the public sector and that meant getting approval from the business office; in the private sector the money belongs to the company, so they could do whatever they want with it, but in the public sector every taxpayer penny is accounted for.

But that didn't stop Victoria from hounding him. Not only that, but then she insisted that she participate in the interviews. Again, a seemingly reasonable request, particularly since she was after all the superintendent. But small requests have large repercussions… especially when Victoria was the hub of every final decision. Thus, nothing could be accomplished while she sat in a meeting, and sometimes interviews could occupy an entire morning.

"Let me get approval from the business office first," Robby said to her over the phone, but that only invited a firestorm of her impatience.

"I want it done, not tomorrow, not today, but yesterday! So why isn't it done already? Are you so negligent that you can't handle one small detail?"

It was harassment, if not hostile, but what could be done? The Board dismissed all allegations, giving her the benefit of the doubt. "But I need to check with them," he replied, trying to cover his butt. "Then I can post it."

"Just have it done! I need that position filled. I tell them how it is and I'm telling you how it is! Now get it done!"

Robby was shaking. For a grown man, he was simply terrified of her, and to make matters worse his office was just a step away from hers. She could literary shout at him if she wanted, but too often she preferred to simply pick up the phone and shout. Even more unsettling was that she called him just to demand his presence in her office. Like a kid being sent to the principal's office, she reprimanded him for at least twenty minutes and then sent him away.

"Do you have any idea how much of an imbecile you are? Do you! I can't stand incompetence and I expect nothing short of your full cooperation. Now get it done!" Stalwart as she was imposing, she silenced everyone who questioned her, including the business office. "I've been a business manager before. I know the money!"

Disillusionment reigned, and where the job used to be enjoyable now nobody looked forward to it. Robby especially. He sighed whenever he got out of his car in the morning. He loathed going to work now, and frankly it showed. He had gained nearly twenty pounds in just a short period of time thanks to Victoria. But no doubt she would simply turn something like that back on him, calling him lazy and unmotivated.

All he wanted, all anybody wanted, was a little bit of gratitude. Was that so much to ask for? Was it also so much to ask to not arrive in the parking lot at the same time as she did, or to be greeted by her smile that changed the second they walked in. The instant they walked in it disappeared and like having split personalities she turned on him. What a way to start the day.

But Victoria was who she was, a royal bitch. But to make matters worse, she hired based on whom she liked, not on expectations, objectives or even competencies. And so, her hires were miniature clones of her, likeminded but also docile to her will. But if being who she was got results, then why not? After all, sometimes it takes a swift hammer to build change.

And so, after having hired three executive assistants, she was now able to triple the flow of paperwork. Emails bombarded everyone's desk, and lunch breaks now came and went without ever being taken; her army of secretaries meant nobody could keep up. And as efficient as they were they were even more coldhearted.

In one instance, a special education teacher called the office to complain. Apparently, he had set aside the gym for his students only to find out that at the last second that it had been reserved for some other purpose. "But I had reserved the gym weeks ago," he said, objecting. But the assistant simply told him to go across the street and use the local church's gym. "It is what it is," she replied. "So I suggest you bend like the wind and be flexible."

"Exactly how do you propose I do that?" he asked resentfully. "I need handicap-accessible vans. That church you're talking about is across a highway, not a street!"

"Then why are you talking to this office," she said, hanging up the phone. "You should be speaking with transportation." Perhaps it is no surprise that the three assistants quickly earned the dub name of the three witches. Every morning they met Victoria in the lobby, waiting for her with a regimented smile and an eagerness to begin. Snobbish and uncaring, they followed her lead to the dot and their purses at their side were like swords at the hip.

Chapter 4

Meeting the New Boss

Shannon checked her email and saw a post from human resources to fill an internal vacancy. At once she leapt from her chair. Not only did it pay better, but it was also in the superintendent's office. How could she turn down a stepping-stone opportunity? Without hesitation she applied for it, happy to leave her current job.

It wasn't that her boss was sexist. He was just lazy, but slothful to the point of annoyance. Once he had her put some heavy boxes into storage that required a stepladder. Unfortunately, there was neither one around nor was he feeling like getting up, so she asked maintenance to bring one over. It arrived while she was at lunch, the boss forgot why it was there and told maintenance to simply take it back; he later apologized, but still didn't help.

As she read over the job description she liked the position even more. First and foremost, there was no lifting of any heavy boxes. Secondly, it involved social media marketing. Perfect! It was a win-win. The fact that she might meet new people was just gravy; she enjoyed her co-workers, but a change of scenery was definitely an order.

Modest, yet ambitious, Shannon worked towards her goals. She was friendly, caring and happy. She didn't stir waters by being opinionated or by competing with her co-workers. Instead, she believed in collaboration, that many hands make light work, and that productivity derived from teamwork; that efficiency was a result of employing the talents of a team, not through the exploitation of labor.

She believed everyone played an important role on a team, but perhaps this is why she clashed with so many bosses, from her current one to her previous at a daycare chain. While the former grumbled at the thought of lifting a helping hand the latter failed to recognize the talents of its team and subsequently filed for bankruptcy; a class action lawsuit was further proof of its blind leadership.

She didn't meant to clash, but time and again her bosses exploited the worker, putting their feet on the desk, reprimanding but never praising, and always took credit for their employees' success. She wasn't looking for a trophy, but a thank you went a long way: at the daycare, she had to clean feces off her arm as well as the baby. It was disgusting, but management neither appreciated her efforts for keeping the children sanitized nor replenished the soap and baby wipes; they were too busy talking about growth. So, she had to buy her own, and for $11 an hour she made sure each baby under her care was well looked after.

She wasn't one to complain. Despite having a Master's Degree she worked where she could, making what she could, hoping the next turn would be better. She believed in "paying her dues," and as she filled out the application she now felt she was finally there.

At the interview, she met Victoria and Robby. The superintendent shook her hand firmly and was as rigid and cold as the white painted cement wall behind them. Robby on the other hand was a giant teddy bear. He pushed his glasses back up with his pudgy fingers and read off his questions with sincere interest in what Shannon had to say; Victoria meanwhile ignored the approved set of legal questions and asked what she wanted, neither caring to Shannon's replies nor sharing any degree of emotion, such as smile.

"Where do you see yourself in five years?" she asked.

Shannon thought for a second. "Well, my goal is to be in a position that fits with my degree. I'm really good at social marketing."

Victoria looked unimpressed, as though her answer was a waste of one's life. "Social media?"

"Uh, yeah. Social media."

"Okay."

Apparently, that open question had a correct answer, which Shannon failed to get. Who knew! But Robby offered her an assuring smile. He valued following one's dreams; it was his biggest regret. Few knew that he dreamed of working in construction, but every influence in his life pushed him away from that, and so he went into human resources.

Victoria meanwhile listened to nobody but herself. She had climbed the ladder not by listening to others but by laughing at those that tried to redirect her; she grabbed her destiny with conviction and refused to let go. That was why she was a superintendent and why someone like Robby took orders.

"If I was to say the deadline for a project was due by the end of the week," she said to Shannon, asking her a few final questions, "then how soon could you get it to me?" What Shannon didn't know was that of all the candidates

Victoria had interviewed thus far, none had lasted as long as she had, and Robby was secretly pleased about that.

"I would certainly try to get it to you early, if I can."

Victoria smiled. That answer she liked. After a few more probing questions, such as her martial status and if Shannon had any children, Victoria excused herself. It wasn't that she had something more pressing to do. It was that she simply meant to imprint her importance onto Shannon. Victoria never finished meetings. She began them.

<u>Chapter 5</u>

Precursor to Disaster

Despite Robby correctly assuming Victoria wished to hire Shannon he was nevertheless scolded for doing so without her consent, a classic catch-22 of her notoriety since she simply expected her subordinates to read her mind.

* * * * * * * *

After sipping his latte and shouting at his agents, Tobias instituted a new policy of fines. Henceforth, anyone with less than three closings a month had to pay $250 a month. Failure to log into the corporate webpage at least once a month, $50; failure to log into the corporate marketing page every 48 hours, $50; failure to update buyer list at sales meeting, $25; and failure to show up at a meeting, $25.

23

"And just to remind all of you," he said. "I think you're all spoiled rotten. Now go out and get me sales."

If internal discontent was escalating so was customer dissatisfaction. Tobias marketed the company with advertisements offering to buy a seller's home if it didn't sell within 120 days. Unfortunately, he rarely if ever kept his word, often telling clients that their floor plan was "weird" or "unusual," or offering other such excuses like, "too rural," or "too unique."

In addition to those ads, he also spent $26,000 on advertising, including $800 on just one website that marketed to realtors, promising larger conversions of leads. But despite being unable to objectify these expenditures, he did manage to personally close about 10 homes a month at 3%, which meant a lucrative commission of $30,000. Certainly, Tobias was doing quite well for himself.

But his success was not shared. Agents came and went, as did office staff. One office assistant lasted only two weeks. But that didn't stop Tobias from insisting she pay her way to a seminar that cost $900.

"Everyone in this office needs to do a hell of a lot better," he said, insisting everyone sign up. "So, if you think you're smart and intelligent and can do this job without expert help then think again. I don't want people who limit themselves. I want people who learn and expand their minds. So, I expect to see everyone's name on this list."

But $900 was a lot of money. So why should anyone spend that if it's just to attend a motivational speaker. How does being motivated help sell homes? "Because," Tobias said, "every tool in a toolbox helps build a building." Which is why he spent tens of thousands of dollars a year on his favorite speaker, a giant in the industry, and had six coaches. "The man's a genius," he liked to say. "I never realized why I do what I do until him."

He also spent $20,000 to do a 30 second commercial with the shark of real estate in Los Angeles, whose company sold for over $65 million. It was room of ego during the shoot. The shark couldn't decide which suit to wear, each one costing a fortune; the shoes alone cost between $400- $2,800.

"Who buys flip-flops for $29?" the shark joked. "I do!" Perhaps it's no surprise then that this person publicly admitted forsaking time with their child to foster their ego. "I tell people, if you don't like me then get out of America, because I'm a locomotive and I'm going to run you over. That's a promise, threat, and guarantee. Welcome to the big leagues."

Chapter 6

Moving Up in the World

Upon learning that Shannon had applied for the position and was being hired her current boss flipped. Feeling inexplicably betrayed, he suddenly accused her of poor performance; perhaps he simply couldn't accept having to lift boxes himself, but whatever the case he abruptly went on a malicious campaign, going so far as to contact Robby and "give a more honest report" of her character.

Was he serious? For a man that barely left his office he was now running around like he was training for the Olympics. "What's going on with you, Shannon? I'm getting reports from students that you're being short with them. We can't have that."

She had no idea what he was talking about, but between her interview and when she received the official letter he slandered her as much as possible. "Let's try and be professional. There's nothing wrong with stacking boxes and greeting students and staff. It's a noble profession and you should be proud to do it. There's no need to apply or accept any other position. You should be happy here."

But she just ignored him. Robby did as well. After all, if Victoria wanted her then why should he question that? He simply told the man politely that the superintendent had made her decision, and if he had a grievance then he should move that through the proper channels; Robby was a teddy bear, but that didn't mean he wasn't assertive. Anytime, a district or department tried to strong-arm the administration he simply reminded them with whom they were talking to. He was the head of HR and he was no subordinate's bitch.

With that the man retreated back to his office like a turtle hiding in his shell. Meanwhile, Shannon received the official news, but her joy was cut short by the pay. The job posting had been for $15 an hour. Now she was being hired in at $11. Had there been a mistake? She instantly called up Robby, who explained that it had been reduced due to budget constraints. "But let me see what I can do," he said. "You did mention you had strong social media marketing skills. Let me see what I can do with that."

Officially, the position was just an administrative assistant role, but that changed after Victoria gave it some more thought. Although at first she had dismissed the idea of social marketing it now seemed like a good idea, especially to market her leadership, and so with her approval Robby was able to increase the pay back to $15 an hour.

Shannon was delighted to hear that and happily gave her two-week's notice. Not surprisingly her boss just gave her a snarky look and closed the door behind him; she couldn't wait to leave. But the following day she received another call from Robby. He had some bad news.

"I wanted to let you know that things have changed, but only slightly," he said, telling her that at that the last second Victoria interceded with a final alteration to the position. Instead of being paid $15 an hour at 40 hours a week, which would have given her benefits, she was instead working part-time for the county; a third party would pay the other half of her time. So, technically she was still 40 hours, but not with the same employer.

This was disappointing to hear, especially since Shannon had student debts to pay and working full time for a non-profit like education meant she was eligible for federal loan forgiveness. Now that was no longer possible.

Robby could hear her despair over the phone, but there was nothing he could do. Victoria had spoken. He waited on the other end while Shannon thought about it. At last, she sighed and accepted. It was still a stepping-stone after all.

Chapter 7

Being Too Efficient

By the end of the day of her new job, Shannon was overwhelmed. It wasn't the superintendent that she had to worry about as much as her unsympathetic entourage. They treated everyone with disdain, issuing deadlines without excuse, and didn't waste time in idle chitchat. Industrial to the core, they worked without break and often through lunch, insisting the same upon others, but then that's the way Victoria treated them, so perhaps it could be excused.

"We have a deadline to meet, Shannon," said one, handing her an assignment. "I need it done by 3 PM." It was already 11 AM. By 11:30 AM the other two had already phoned her as well, making it apparent that whatever she was doing was less important than their request; by 1 PM she was called into the superintendent's office.

"I understand you're not getting your work done," Victoria said, stopping Shannon before the young woman had a chance to explain herself. "Let me speak. I don't have time for any immature excuses. I'm going to explain how it's done here and you're going to listen. When I finish I don't want you to speak. I just want you to get up, go to your desk, and get things done."

Shannon was taken aback. Immature excuses! Was she serious? Suddenly Shannon wasn't so sure about having accepted the job, but before 3 PM she was once again in the office being scolded. It was unbelievable. She was trying to finish, but apparently she wasn't fast enough; their disregard was as exasperating as it was exhausting. Who could work in such an environment? But to add icing to the cake, they wished her a good night at the end of the day, as though it wasn't personal. It sure felt that way.

Nevertheless, Shannon worked diligently and by the end of the week had not only figured things out, but was surprising the crows by finishing her work early. Now it was their turn to be taken aback. They tried to issue her more, even stacking projects on each other, but she finished them with such efficiency that it was now their turn to fall behind.

While the secretaries received Victoria's scorn, Shannon earned her praise. They resented it, but what could they do? The young woman was simply more efficient.

"I need triplicate copies of this report," said one, following right behind another. They handed her work one after the next, hoping to slow her down, but Shannon only frustrated their attempts.

It wasn't that she was being retaliatory. Shannon was simply adapting, using her skills to survive. The fact that she was simply more efficient wasn't her fault; after all, that's what the secretaries wanted. They just didn't realize anyone could be so efficient… and Victoria noticed. By the end of the month, Shannon was taking instruction directly from her.

All of a sudden the weight shifted. Now it was Shannon who was able to dictate terms. "I will be happy to do that for you as soon as I finish this for Victoria," she said. But what could they do but accept? Any direction from Victoria was after all priority.

And so, having largely figured things out, Shannon relaxed a bit. She prepared materials for the superintendent, marketed on social media, and tended to the carping ladies, and for three months everything seemed in order. Then one day Robby called her into his office. He said it was for her ninety-day performance review, but as soon as she entered his office she sensed there was something else going on: he seemed on edge, as though deeply troubled. He didn't say what but something was on his mind.

"I'd like to show you a few things if you like, about human resources?" His voice was a bit nervous, and he spoke in riddles so that whatever was bothering him he conveyed through subtlety, through what he offered to show her, as though whatever discovery he had made was not one he wanted to make.

Shannon agreed, and for the next several weeks he began showing her HR, starting with how to organize files. She learned where to input data into the computer, how to sort files, and even learned the software as well as he when he extended her confidential access. Bit by bit, she began to understand human resources just as well as she did social media, but at no time did she tell Victoria. She didn't see the need. After all, she was getting her work done. What harm came from learning something new?

After a month his demeanor had improved, and yet he was still a bit edgy. Whatever was bothering him he did a great job of hiding it. Shannon wanted to inquire but felt it would only exacerbate things, so she didn't. Robby however, read her mind and finally admitted what was bothering him:

A. Ruben

He was overwhelmed. Victoria set unrealistic time frames for his work that were simply impossible to keep pace. That was why he had her learn how to organize and file, input data and even schedule and conduct interviews on his behalf. It was all he could do to stay one step ahead; overwhelmed was an understatement though. From the second he came in Victoria unloaded a week's worth onto him and expected it all done by 9 AM.

He could scarcely eat his lunch in peace without being bombarded by phone or email. In five minutes, Victoria one sent him fifteen emails; she delegated everything. This left her time to send more emails and impress the Board. While everyone else hustled she took all the credit, receiving the Board's adulation, and yet she never once thanked an employee for his or her efforts, including Robby. Until one day, when she asked Shannon into her office.

"I believe you're doing an excellent job here," she said, surprising Shannon as well as everyone else in the office, including the secretaries, who were appalling taken aback. "And I want to help you advance your skills. Tell me what you know and this way I can see how I can help."

What Shannon didn't realize was that she was fishing. Word of her efficiency had reached the superintendent's office and Victoria meant to discover just how much efficient she was and what she knew… the only person not running around like a chicken with its head cut off was Shannon, and while she took this as a compliment it was a red flag for someone like Victoria who was trying to be discreet; the best way to cloak one's actions is to distract others, and it seemed Shannon couldn't be distracted. She was too on top of things.

"I can't thank you enough for sharing with me this morning," she said after Shannon spoke. "You've been a big help. I look forward to hearing more from you."

Chapter 8

Contradictions and Surveys

Upon returning from another "executive retreat," Tobias and Roxy hit the ground running. Inspired by their favorite motivational speaker, they had spent the last few days discovering their destiny; it was an unforgettable date with destiny as the lights, sounds, high-level energy, and people drinking the Kool-Aid was simply irresistible. They absorbed the feel-good "fluff" of lofty words, jumped up and down, gave back rubs, and felt renewed with a tremendous sense of upbeat and positivity; their serotonin was at its apex of this almost religious awakening; they felt lifted, soaring higher than the clouds. It was nothing short of a rock concert for the 99% of people wanting desperately to become the illusionary 1%.

"You can't just go halfway," said Roxy to a friend, "You got to go all the way." She encouraged all of her friends to attend. "It's worth the money. Besides, we encourage all of our employees to do it and that's what makes our office a great place to work."

Of course, the instant they entered the office he stared down at the dirt in the entryway. "What the hell is this doing on the front mat? Is anyone going to pick up this shit?" Everyone had had high hopes, but apparently his retreat hadn't changed him one bit. The only one laughing was Roxy.

"They think they're the 1% like us."

When the receptionist tried to be nice and greet them, Roxy brushed her aside. "Why aren't you working? I don't pay you to stand around."

"Sorry, I was just trying to be nice."

"You're fired. Get out," she interrupted. "And that goes for the rest of you. The only two people that matter in this room are he and I, not any of you. You work for us. That's it. This isn't a nursery where we hold hands and have snack breaks together. The only two people that have any purpose in life are us. We have the mindset of champions, not you. We run the show, not you. Now back to work!"

Then the two went into the conference room to call up one of their six coaches. They deliberately left the door open so everyone could hear.

"Good morning to you, and before we start let's first take a pulse. How are you feeling and what goals have you set for the day?" According to the website, every coach was hand-selected and trained by the "father of coaching" himself, this guru. Each had to participate in at least 250 hours of yearly training in the same strategies, tools and methods that the guru emphasized to millions' of people.

"We're feeling fantastic," Tobias said. "It was an amazing journey we just had and we can't wait to do it again, but as we walked in this morning I felt drained by our employees and their problems. How can we walk in tomorrow morning without that?"

The coach was confused. "You mean how can you share your excitement with them?"

"No. How can we walk in and not feel bombarded by our employees? I want to feel good, not depressed."

"Well, one way is to invite your office to attend the next workshop. We have many companies that bring their employees to help build a stronger work environment."

"Yeah, that sounds expensive, and I don't really want to spend money on them. I just want to not hear their problems anymore. What advice do you have for that?"

The coach tried again. "Have you tried developing an intimate working relationship with your office staff, understanding their needs and helping them is a great way to begin the process of self-empowerment. Thus, allowing you the freedom to grow your business."

"I can grow my business no problem. It's just their constant nagging. I honestly feel like I've hired babies."

"Perhaps that's an area we need to revisit then. Hiring the right people is an essential part of growing. After all, we don't necessarily want to be just excellent. We want to be outstanding, and that includes those we hire. We want to have outstanding employees."

Roxy interjected. "Let me cut in here. I think what my husband is trying to say is that success belongs to us, not our employees. After all, this is our business, not theirs. They're just simply here to get a paycheck. So, how can we get them to smile everyday, because I don't want to come to my office everyday and see frowns."

The coach was speechless. The entire point of the speaker's message was unleashing the power within one's self, discovering their limitless possibilities, and achieving success where barriers once existed. It was a process, not an instant transformation; although the guru made it seem simple and straightforward there was in reality a great deal of work in reconstructing one's personal blueprints: people inherently limit themselves, he would say at workshops. The goal is to recognize what limitations a person has and break through.

For instance, a person living on the streets may believe he or she will never escape that world. That's a limitation. An employee who feels they will never become Employee of the Month is a limitation. Anytime someone uses the word "never" they are limiting themselves, but to Tobias and Roxy they believed such a journey was reserved to only the most exceptional. Everyone else was just a peon.

"Why don't we do this," the coach finally said. "Let's put together a survey, a team work assessment if you will, which will give us some insight into how your employees are feeling."

"But I don't care about how they feel," she said.

"Then consider it as a measure of your culture."

After several revisions, and strong suggestions by the coach to reword certain loaded questions, the two issued the survey to everyone. They were to be answered with Strongly Agree, Agree, Indifferent, Disagree or Strongly Disagree. Among the questions included the following:

1.   There is a culture of personal responsibility within the team, so blaming and shaming is non-existent.

2.   I am, as a member of the team, encouraged to innovate new ideas.

3.   The company recognizes my achievements.

4.   The overall physical office environment contributes to my health and state of mind.

5.   There are clear, effective conflict resolution skills practiced by the team.

6.   There is a negative aspect of our team culture at work that people generally don't see or admit.

The word "emotional" was omitted from the fourth question, because otherwise Roxy refused to include it. The survey was issued to everyone and despite the coach's strong advice that it be anonymous, Tobias and Roxy insisted that employees put their name on it. Not surprisingly, several were fired as a result… and almost always because of the last question. One agent, seeing the writing on the wall, wrote, "Open Your EYES."

A. Ruben

The Numbers

<u>Chapter 9</u>

Running the Numbers

Victoria reported an astounding surplus of almost $460,000, which surprised the Board. They were ecstatic, and at once shook her hand in celebration. "Congratulations," they said, issuing her praise and adulations. But was it deserved? After all, how does one jump from $80,000 in projected surplus to nearly half a million dollars?

There was concern from a few, but they were voiced over. "The fact remains that the superintendent has done an outstanding job here. This should be commended, not condemned," said the Chair. But if anyone should have raised a red flag it should have been him. Instead, he approved her raise of $6 an hour, bringing her salary to just over $161,000.

But how could anyone be so imprudent as to not even consider the possibility of error? After all, such a jump certainly warranted a second look, especially in a county with rising costs; in her annual report, Victoria informed the public of everything happening, from professional development workshops to community outreach programs, such as adolescent pregnancy and drug awareness, and interestingly enough the number of funding required from year to the next seemingly increased. So again, how does one jump so high when costs are rising?

But Victoria was a talker, and so whenever there were questions she simply manipulated the conversation to safer shores. Several years ago, she was challenged for authorizing one-seventh of the budget to be spent on a top brand leadership-training program. At its core, the program was about how to win friends and influence others, but why spend one-seventh of the budget on it, and why limit such an expensive resource to just one school that happened to be for high school dropouts?

"Every child deserves a chance," she said at the time, "and we can't leave any child behind."

"They dropped out," a board member said in objection. "Frankly, he or she had their chance!"

"That is true," a second replied. "But even still, to devote such a huge expense to high school dropouts when achieving students in our other schools can't receive this training behooves me. After all, this is practically corporate training. Shouldn't our best and brightest be receiving this training just as well?"

Victoria couldn't agree more, but added that appropriate protocol had been followed. "Nevertheless, I am happy to oblige this board's decision, but can we afford it? Can we continue this program for all of our students." They couldn't and so it was stopped. Not surprisingly, the statistics of the high school dropouts collapsed.

But was Victoria blamed? Hardly. Instead the blame was put on a lower administrator who had been in charge of the program. As it turned out this administrator's husband happened to work for the corporate training, which did not help her situation; to make matters worse, her husband was a junior partner, which only made the apparent corruption all that much worse. Victoria was hailed a hero.

But how could she talk her way out of such a jump now? Already there were loud voices even if it was just from a few board members. "Can you please explain how?" a female board member asked insistently. She never liked Victoria and was hoping this might be the opportunity to strike and put an end to her reign once and for all.

Victoria just smiled and praised the woman on being fiscally astute.

"Cut the crap," the woman said, interrupting her. She was an older lady, who had served on the Board for years.

"I can see you're direct. I like that," she replied. "And to answer you this is a preliminary budget report, not an annual report. We are expecting this, but anything can happen. I believe it is important to hope for the best, but expect the worst. So, while we can celebrate we are still not out of the storm yet."

"So then why are we reviewing this report at all, when it is completely unrealistic?"

"Again," she said calmly, using the woman's hostility against her. "As everyone is quite aware we are in the midst of a nationwide recession and this means tightening our belts all around, but to see progress of any kind is, in my belief, a relief, and just as I request updates from my administration team so I feel the need to update this board's members. I believe communication in times like these is just as important as a bit of good news."

As the room applauded her, the woman folded her arms in disgust. Victoria had as many friends as she had enemies; she certainly had more of the latter online, from all those she ever terminated. But the fact that she was also a member of the Board only helped her position more.

Chapter 10

Unexplained Expenses

During the corporate training scandal, a board member resigned in disgust. "Confidence is developed by success," he said, resenting Victoria's attitude. She said he was entitled to his opinion but that every child deserves a future. He disagreed, "You can't be taught to succeed. You have to study hard and fight for it. I should know. I'm an attorney."

* * * * * * * *

Of all of her subordinates with access to the numbers, Robby was the most alarmed. Victoria had the most of any reimbursed expenses, exceeding anyone by 11 times; she claimed $65,500 and the next highest was the former assistant superintendent at just above $5,000.

"What the hell is going on here?" he said to himself, forgetting that Shannon was nearby.

"Everything okay?"

"Ah, yeah," he said, trying to pretend it was nothing.

"You sure? You look really stressed out."

"Yeah, of course. No, I'm fine."

But he couldn't understand how anyone had $65,500 in reimbursed expenses. After all, how much was gas? Lodgings? Even conferences couldn't possibly be that much, and besides whenever she was invited to speak the host paid for everything. So then what was it? What explained her astronomical number? He couldn't figure it out.

According to the county's reimbursement policy, the Board was responsible for approving any expenses of staff to professional meetings. The Board or its designee approved any overnight travel prior to being incurred; no individual could approve his or her own travel or traveling expenses.

Moreover, only the Board could approve "actual and necessary expenses" of any professional staff member within the course of performing his or her services, which had to be under the direction of the Board and in accordance with the Superintendent. This seemed to in order expect for a later statement that seemed to offer a loophole. "Any reimbursement for other job-related expenses shall be approved by the Superintendent."

If it wasn't gas, lodgings or conferences then what was it? If the average employee's reimbursed expenses were only $3,600 then what exactly constituted Victoria's? Surely to anyone this amount warranted suspicion, and as a matter of fact a later investigation did question it but found nothing out of the ordinary. In fact, it found her behavior in good standing!

But Robby did know, at least as much as it was submitted to him on paper. And yet, to whom could he tell? To whom could he convey his concerns? Certainly not the business office, because they complied with Victoria's ever request; the Chief Financial Officer (CFO) would later deny any misconduct, citing everything had been done consistently with "past practices." And the assistant superintendent had already resigned. This left only the Board, but Victoria had them right where she wanted them.

Chapter 11

Getting in Deep

In the majority- if not all- reimbursement policies across the nation Board approval is required in all circumstances. Even the Board President is accountable to the Board. The loophole Victoria used was not only unique in its inclusion, but was also its own paragraph in the policy.

* * * * * * * *

"Shannon, can you come into my office," Victoria said. Her tone over the phone was happy, and she greeted her with a smile. "How are you doing today?"

"I'm good. Thank you."

"Wonderful, and I see Robby is helping you out. I hope you're learning a lot."

"Yes, I am."

"I'm so glad to hear that. Care to share with me what things you're learning? I'm curious how I can help as well."

Naïvely, she shared. But then why should she suspect anything? Victoria had a reputation in the office, but despite her stern approach she was interested in her employee's wellbeing, at least that's how it appeared.

"Well, I'm learning a lot about human resources, how to do the paperwork, keep it organized, and putting it into the computer system."

"Even the computer system! I'm impressed. Please go on," she said, listening attentively as Shannon then explained how Robby was having her participate in interviews and even run a few. "That's tremendous responsibility. I'm glad to hear you're able to tackle such tasks."

She blushed. "I'm just trying to help out where I can."

"Well, you're doing a marvelous job. I'm so glad you shared with me. Thank you for your time." Shortly afterwards, Robby was fired.

Shannon didn't understand why. Was it something she had said? She didn't know, but as her workload suddenly increased she had little time to contemplate it.

Without Robby the human resources department was shaken indefinitely, and many turned to Shannon for answers. Despite being just an administrative assistant, she had casually interacted with others, unwittingly building a reputation for herself as someone who was efficient and decisive; not surprisingly the department instantly turned to her for leadership when they heard the news of his dismissal.

Now all at once, she was the de facto interim manager of Human Resources. Although Victoria eventually hired a replacement, many still considered Shannon to be in charge; and the replacement was anything but friendly.

Meanwhile, Robby's termination had raised alarm, giving ammunition to Victoria's enemies on the Board. At a cost of $45,000, the investigation ruled Victoria had acted appropriately. She alleged her head of HR was simply under-performing and they bought it.

Chapter 12

Taking on Water

Bitter but not beaten, Victoria's rivals on the Board continued to push for a financial inquiry. "But it was just a preliminary report," said another Board member. They just looked at him repulsively. "Exactly how naïve are you?"

* * * * * * * *

Despite her workload, Shannon performed beautifully. Far from infallible, she made mistakes but unlike others she owned them, which not only separated her from others but also earned the respect of her peers, who were instantly taken aback by such accountability; the typical response when someone faulted was to blame another, but not Shannon. She accepted the blame, learned from it, and contrarily to most fears soared even higher.

She was at first warned to not take the blame, but she ignored that, insisting that if the fault were hers then she would own it. "That's your funeral," a manager said from another department, urging her to not commit career suicide so early on. "Seriously though, you really should not take the blame if it can be avoided. I'm just saying." But Shannon just thanked him for his advice and continued forward.

Even the new HR manager that replaced Robby began to inexplicably reprimand her, starting with verbal warnings on her "inappropriate role," as de facto manager.

"I'm just doing my job," she said, unsure how her efficiency and productivity were at fault. If anything, she was raising the standard.

"Your production isn't in question," the woman replied. "It's your attitude. I'm just letting you know that you need to work on it."

"My attitude?" What was the lady talking about? Nearly everyone already complimented her on her friendly demeanor. "Are you saying I'm too friendly?"

"Oh my goodness no! It's the opposite. I'm urging you to work on being friendly. Right now you're very cold."

Wait, what! Where was this coming from? "I'm sorry. I'm cold?"

"Yes," she replied unmoved, "and it's come to my attention that this has created a very hostile environment among others. So, consider this your verbal warning. We're addressing this now and I expect you will work on it."

Stunned, she didn't know what to say. Was she serious? How on earth did she come to that conclusion, but it wasn't over. In fact, this was only the beginning.

A week later she was once again called into the woman's office. "I thought we had addressed this," she began, irate at her. "Now I hear you're sidestepping the chain of command. I don't understand why, but frankly I'm not interested in excuses. I'm just letting you now this is your second warning. There will not be a third and I will be informing the superintendent of your misconduct."

Misconduct? "I guess I'm confused. I'm getting my work done, but you're saying things I haven't done. So, either I'm not aware of my behavior or there's some confusion about my role in this office."

"I'm letting you know where you stand."

"Well, I think the best course of action here is to speak with my boss, Victoria, and sort this out. I feel that somehow I've inexplicably let you down as well as others and I will speak with her on how I can correct this."

"She's busy right now."

"Oh, I know. I create her schedule. I know when she's free and when she's not." With that, she walked out.

What Shannon didn't know then was why Victoria had hired the woman. As it turned out, of all the candidates this woman was more "in line with policy." Unlike Robby, who questioned the reimbursed expenses she signed them off without hesitation; later discovery revealed annuity payments being allowed to pay for Victoria's loans. Apparently, she cleared the first $13,638 unreservedly.

Chapter 13

Ramming into the Iceberg

Elsewhere, Tobias was correcting his agent. "Don't ever say yeah or yep, say yes. People judge you by what you say. I don't ever want to hear you say yep or yeah again." Suddenly, Roxy called him over. "Yeah, what do you need?"

* * * * * * * *

With Robby's dismissal the Board came under intense pressure for answers. Apparently, Robby had friends just like anyone, but unknown to Victoria his friends had influence and they wanted justice. Now all of a sudden, the allies of Victoria had no choice but to approve a financial investigation. Although Victoria was neither accused of any misconduct nor resisted in cooperating with the audit she was placed on paid administrative leave until the matter as resolved.

As the auditors began sorting through the files they discovered a series of discrepancies that while not illegal were perhaps not ethical. And yet, apparently the practices had been going on for some time and thus were labeled as "past practices." Among these included annuity payments being substituted with payments towards student loans; while this practice of substitution wasn't necessarily unlawful the fact that two year's worth of payments were made in the same year did raise a red flag.

But the red ran greater than that. As the audit team dug deeper they found that not only had the new HR manager approved it but so had the CFO of the business office as well as several members of the Board. The latter vehemently denied any responsibility, noting that Victoria's contract neither allowed nor prohibited it and thus they had committed no wrongdoing.

Yet, what stunned the auditors was how many people were involved. While reinvested, annuities are tax-exempt, but once distributed they became taxable income. This should only affect the individual, but for whatever reason the business office, the CFO, and several board members made it their business too. Thus, what could have been presumably an excusable reason was now raising eyebrows. Why were so many people involved? It wasn't necessarily unlawful, but undoubtedly there were some ethical issues at hand, so was there a whistleblower among them?

Everything came back to Robby. While it couldn't be proven that his dismissal was related to knowledge of what was going on it certainly seemed that way. As head of HR, Robby did know what the reimbursed expenses were as well as the substitution payments, but his refusal to comply more than likely brought about his termination; Victoria was renowned for firing anyone who objected with her policies and certainly Robby fell into that category.

While Victoria claimed dismissal of staff was for "fiscal efficacy," the objections from her enemies said otherwise. While undoubtedly biased, her opponents and those adversely affected by her decisions pointed to a sharp increase in terminations since her inception:

From her start date, Victoria had laid off 74 support staff, replacing them with one full-time employee and 3 part-time. The unions at first had tried to negotiate, but against ultimatums communications eventually broke down and Victoria got her way; the fact that Robby was administration and therefore not in the union only made his position that more fragile.

In another purge, she dismissed 24 employees, who happened to be special education staff. This allegation by the public proved correct with findings by the audit team as they began investigating the Special Education fund. They found that it had in fact been reduced while the remaining two funds had meanwhile increased.

But this was only the tip of the iceberg. The further the team dug the worst the picture got. It was one thing to claim "fiscal efficacy." That at least could be somewhat accepted in a recession, but then giving out raises was inexcusable, especially when referring to it as, "supplemental funds." Victoria was subsequently put on suspension.

Ironically, she once spoke at a conference on salaries and the value of performance-based compensation. The team found raises went as low as 5.6% to its highest of 12.4%. Thus, in taking a step back it seemed as though Victoria had rewarded her loyal "enthusiasts" while eliminating those that voiced any objections.

Awed and shocked, the team then began to probe into her preliminary report and its audacious $460,000. Was there any validity in this? Considering the basic math right in front of them it didn't take long for the audit team to discover the impossibility of her claim:

If Victoria saved the county about $250,000 by cutting Special Education then how on earth did she generate such a high estimate when the other two funds were increased? It didn't make any sense. In fact, the math was so elementary it was sickening.

The Budget	*Yearly Change*
The General Fund & The Vocational Services Fund	($900,000)
Special Education Fund	$250,000

How on earth did she claim savings of nearly half a million dollars when clearly the budget change was in the red?

From a poor preliminary report to ethical questions to unexplained reimbursements the Board came under intense pressure from the community when the news finally broke; the fact that the county paid nearly $65,000 for the audit team- almost as much as Victoria's reimbursement expenses- drew even more outcry from the public. What exactly was going on with the education system in their community!

Chapter 14

Adaptation is Survival

With Victoria suddenly under investigation the dominoes came tumbling down. All at once, a handful of employees in the business office quit, the CFO resigned, and five district administrators resigned that all happened to be close acquaintances with her. In addition, several other administrators resigned after trying to promote ethical leadership, but couldn't "rightfully" accept a pay cut.

* * * * * * * *

When the new head of HR also resigned, Shannon also decided it was time for her to leave. Although many pleaded for her to stay including the three secretaries, she felt it was time. She had enjoyed working with Robby as well as everyone else, but her talents had largely been suppressed or scrutinized. She had been hired as an administrative assistant and for social media marketing, but neither Victoria nor the recent head of HR would permit anything to be published without undergoing intense scrutiny. In one instance, a simple brochure was too "kid friendly." Another time, she was asked to redo a marketing design, because the HR manager disliked the color purple.

"Please reconsider Shannon," said a friendly co-worker. "Considering what's going on around here I'm pretty sure some good positions will open up. You could be in a really good spot for a promotion."

Shannon slept on it, but decided to move on. It wasn't that Victoria was under investigation or that she had been a difficult boss. She just felt the environment was too unstable; although she suspected Victoria had manipulated her she simply wanted to move on and find another job that could utilize her talents more often.

While her adversities celebrated her downfall, proclaiming it as karma, Shannon applied for a job opening with a real estate firm and received an enthusiastic call from Tobias. He was delighted to meet someone with her talents.

Chapter 15

Being #1 on Google Search

"I've been looking for someone with your talents," Tobias said, so excited he had to stand in the interview. "What this place needs is to get painted across the Internet and I think you can do it. Say yes and I promise you won't regret it." His office was spacious and clearly had signs of growing. There were new desks being set up and agents were coming in and out the entire time she was there; unlike the Superintendent's Office it was a place that was growing.

"So what do you think," he asked. "Can I begin to move you in?"

She was still taken aback. She had never had an employer beg her before, so this was definitely a new experience. Nevertheless, she wanted to consider his offer.

"Not a problem. Take your time. Just let me know by tomorrow morning or I'll find someone else." It came off like a threat, but by the way he was smiling it seemed almost casual. Creepy casual.

As she stepped out the door to her car though she got a text. It was from Tobias. Wait, what! She had just left his office and he was already texting her. I mean she had her phone number on her résumé, but what employer reached out that fast? She had literary just stepped off the curb into the parking lot. "We would love to see you on Tuesday." It was Monday.

At a starting pay of $16, the first task Tobias gave her was to paint the company all over social media. It was a colossal task, especially since the only marketing tool the company had was Facebook. "Okay, no problem," she said, ready to take on the challenge.

"One last thing though," he said. "I understand that on Bing and Google we are not listed as number one. I did a search of us and we're not even on the first page. Do me a favor and call up Bing and Google and get that fixed."

Shannon looked surprised. "Um, that's not really how it works."

"Look it just takes a phone call. See what you can do about taking care of it today. Thanks."

"Wait, no, I mean, that's not possible. I mean that's not how it works at all." She was completely baffled by his request. Did he not know how search engines work? Did he seriously think it only took a phone call to move up?

"I need you to fix this. Can you do it?"

"Yes, but…"

"Great!"

"No, wait, you don't understand. I can't"

"But you just said you can. Now you can't."

She tried to explain how words and phrases fed search engines, how blogs and algorithms worked, and how to find and follow customers online with content-driven articles and compelling topics that stirred emotion. She tried to explain in the most simplistic way possible how audience-focused issues persuaded back and forth dialogue, which added a personal touch; how being "human" was ideal for a company trying to draw in more customers.

"When others like your content they'll share it and link it to other sites like blogs, which is what signals Google and Bing. Whether you're tweeting or blogging, search engines pick up on that. The more it's talked about the higher it goes on the list."

Tobias listened, but it clearly went in one ear and out the other. "I'm hearing a lot of scrabble and static. Let's try and convert that to making a phone call."

She struggled to get him to understand. "But that's not how it works."

"You can't make a phone call?"

"No, I can make phone calls, but that's not going to get us anywhere. If anything they'll laugh."

"Laughing? Who's laughing?"

"No, that's not what I mean. I mean Google and Bing will laugh, because that's not how it works. You can't just call them up and ask to be number one on their search engine."

"Who's asking? I just want it done."

Was he serious? At first she thought he was, but now she just couldn't believe it. Tobias truly had no idea how any of it worked.

"Why can't you just call up Bing and make us #1?"

"Because that's not how it works!" Now she was getting frustrated, and this was only the first day.

"Then just go into their system and make it happen."

"Wait, what! You want me to do what?"

"It's simple. Do your nerd thing and hack into Google and Bing and make it happen." The fact that he even knew the word 'hack' amazed her, but was he serious?

"Just so I understand what you're asking me to do. You want me to hack into Google and Bing and magically have this company's listings be number one?"

"That doesn't sound very loyal to me," he said, not liking her tone. "I know you can fix this. I didn't hire you because you were dumb."

"I'm not dumb, but I'm trying to explain how search engines work and hacking into Google and Bing is definitely not the way to do it, not to mention illegal."

"Oh, please. There's nothing wrong with ripping a page out of a dictionary and taping it to the front."

Chapter 16

Bulldozing the Competition

For the first month, Shannon judged whether this had been a good decision. Tobias was completely oblivious to how social media worked, but when it came to real estate he was astute, selling low-end $50,000 homes to as high as $600,000. Nevertheless, his management style left much to be desired... she quickly understood why there were so many vacant desks, which she had mistakenly thought were new desks during her interview.

The turnover was unreal. Agents came and went just as often as Tobias checked his face and suit in the mirror near the coffee pot, which was for clients only... per Roxy. But as clueless as Tobias was about social media and the tenure of his employees his wife was nefarious for nitpicking and faultfinding.

"Don't touch the glass," she said to an office assistant that put her hand on the desk. It wasn't her desk, but the assistant's. Every desk had a glass top, but nobody was allowed to put his or her skin on it. "There's no slouching on the job, so I shouldn't see your arms resting when you type."

She nitpicked and he cursed, and together they screamed as often as the weather changed, badgering both employees and each other with criticism. "Just keep telling yourself you're the best, mister hotshot! You're nothing but a second-hand bookstore."

"What are talking about woman? I am the best. I am the greatest! What do you bring to this office? All I see is a mountain of jewels."

"And you pay for all of them, so don't give me crap about them. You want to buy them for me, fine! I'll wear them."

"Don't wear them then!"

"Like hell I won't wear them. I love jewelry!"

"I can see that! Everyone can see that. Hell, the government's satellites can see that."

Every day was a contest of wits between Tobias and Roxy, creating both a hostile work environment as well as plenty of lunch break conversation pieces... and employees learned very quickly to take lunches together to avoid being singled out; strength in numbers was undeniably a survival strategy at Tobias and Roxy's firm.

Everyday, Tobias kicked another competitor to the curb, not carrying if the man or woman had to turn to food stamps to survive. "If you can't stand the heat then get out of the kitchen," he often said. As a broker, he could list, buy and sell, earning him higher commission and gave him more command of his market in terms of how he executed strategy.

In real estate, agents report to a broker, which is someone who has continued his or her education and earned a broker license. This gives a broker greater flexibility in being his or her own boss; Tobias was not only a broker, but also the owner, which gave him even more elasticity. "This is America dammit! If you don't like working under me then find yourself another job. Otherwise get out there and make me money."

With $20 million in annual sales it was no wonder why Tobias marketed himself as one of the top 100 real estate agents in the country, going so far as to have that published on the wall of an internationally renowned newspaper journal; whatever street he walked on he sold. He was #1 in market share; #1 in agent ranking; and #1 for at least the past five years. If he fell to second he fired until his ranking rose, believing that purging acted as a motivator.

And yet for all his success, Tobias's Achilles heel remained marketing. He could unquestionably sell, but pitching his company online simply eluded him; he certainly recognized its value, though the basic mechanics escaped his understanding. He nevertheless hired marketing specialists, particularly young people with skill in technology and social media. Marketing was never his forte, but to his credit he accepted that, admitting he could not punish for what he didn't understand: he was ignorant of how technology worked, but unlike others in the office he extended Shannon a certain degree of immunity.

She was direct with him. At first, she had hesitated, unsure of how to approach his mannerisms, but then after consulting her brother and hearing his pains with a vice-president, she realized she would simply put her foot down and if Tobias didn't like it then so what. She had had enough of incompetent bosses trying to tell her what to do.

"I'd like a raise," she said after three months. Tobias had called her into the conference room for a performance review with Roxy.

"Impossible," he said. "You haven't done anything! It's asinine to reward someone who hasn't done a thing."

She dropped him a look of shame. "Actually I have, and here's what I've done for you." She regularly updated him, but suspected his objection had much more to do with Roxy than anything else; she vehemently opposed raises. "Before you were only on Facebook, but what good is a page if nobody visits it, much like having an open house that no one attends. So, I've been advertising for you, drawing people to the website and a result generating leads."

Roxy laughed. "Oh please. I know better than that. There's no way to prove it. Nice try sweetie, but there's no correlation between bringing people to our website and what leads are generated."

"I just ask," she replied undaunted.

"What do you mean you just ask?"

"Well, you hired me to do the online marketing but also to fill a receptionist role. Since I can do a duel-role this was one of the reasons you told me you hired me. And since I answer the phone I simply ask how they heard about us."

"And they say Facebook?" Tobias said, now taking her side.

"That's just one. I've also got us on Twitter, Pinterest, Reddit, Instagram, just to name a few. The more you're seen and heard about the more the phone rings." And in fact the phone had been off the hook lately, so much so that agents were overwhelmed with leads.

"That doesn't mean the leads are any good," she snapped back.

"I filter them on the phone."

"What do you mean you filter? You don't know how to do that. You're just here to answer the phones and do magic card tricks."

Shannon looked surprised. Was she for real? "Well, I certainly don't know what you mean by magic card tricks, but I do know how to market online and show my results objectively. I filter on the phone to disqualify any poor leads; just because it's a lead doesn't necessarily mean it's a good lead." She learned that from her brother. "Besides, time is money and there's no reason to waste it chasing down poor leads. Let's get the sale and move onto the next one."

Tobias was sold. Shannon may not have been a saleswoman, but she certainly had the confidence and the fortitude to pitch her argument. But Roxy still had some fight in her.

"We didn't give raises to the so-called marketing experts before you. So I don't see any reason to give you one."

"Except for all the reasons I just gave? Whoever came before me hardly did anything in comparison. I have not only promoted the company's image, but the leads I generated resulted in closed sales." That was a good distinction. Being able to create leads is one thing, but to close the sale, especially a profitable sale is far more important, and Shannon began to list of some major accounts that closed as a direct result of her marketing. The proof was right in the pudding and Roxy couldn't deny it then.

Shannon explained how she had been working closely with the agents, getting feedback on their clients and any progress on the leads. To hear about her leads being closed was a nice feeling of accomplishment.

"Alright," Roxy finally said. "But if we give you a raise I want more from you. I want to you schedule showings; you're to carry a phone with you day and night and if I call you then you better answer. You're also going to map routes and figure out the driving directions so people don't get lost. I don't want any excuses from clients or our agents."

Shannon agreed and for that additional workload she received a raise of $1 an hour. It disappointed her. She had tried for at least $3, but Roxy wouldn't have it; not only was she unyielding to a raise, but she took her resentment out on two employees, firing them. The next day, Shannon received $100 bonus for the pay period. "I hope it was worth it to you," Roxy said, whipping it at her.

Chapter 17

Reaching the Top

In the six months since she started, Shannon was able to present a series of statistics to Tobias and Roxy, including the relationship between leads from marketing campaigns and closing rates, which sites generated the most leads, and even the hours of the day that customers inquired. Nevertheless, Tobias continued to pay $6,000 a year for one site, simply because it was popular.

"Everyone uses it," he said.

"That may be, but that doesn't mean buyers are coming from it," she objected as politely as she could. "Just because someone is a buyer doesn't necessarily mean he or she is a good buyer or even a buyer at all." The website was a window into a store. It listed millions of real estate and rental properties as well as gave valuable information, such as the nearby schools and anticipated home expenses.

The reason why Tobias paid $6,000 a year for it was because this way he could be listed as an agent for potential buyers to call. The more he paid the higher on the list he was. And yet, calls made into the office were often poor leads, resulting in both a significant loss of time and money; high agent turnover was a direct consequence.

Moreover, a lack of filtering in the office also meant that whatever lead came in was fiercely competed for, like a pack of dogs fighting over a bone. Although Tobias's agents were in theory on the same team the reality was that it was every man and woman for him or herself; there was little to no cooperation, and Tobias only exacerbated that by seizing leads away from his agents, believing this kept his agents "hungry" and thus more driven.

"I'm not going to stop paying for it," he said, kindly dismissing her. "Potential buyers are as good as any buyer, and the fact that I know that and you don't is why I'm in charge and give the orders around here."

But in addition to his snatching away leads this mentality further stagnated his agent's income. On average, the agents closed 3-4 homes a month. At 3% commission this wasn't necessarily bad, particularly when their cut was easily in the range of $8,000 - $12,000. However, since his agents were all 10-99 employees this meant that at least a third of that income had to be set aside for taxes. Nonetheless, that still left the agent with a sizeable amount. Unfortunately, that was all he or she was ever going to make; three was the minimum, but four was the maximum. Tobias snatched away the rest, and his new fee policy for those selling less than three homes only hurt the agent's pockets more.

Chapter 18

Stagnant Pond Water

With the details of the investigation intensifying, the Board of Education accepted Victoria's resignation. In addition to a severance pay of nearly $86,000, the Board also agreed to 18 months of medical benefits. According to a press release, they agreed to these terms to "avoid potential costly litigation."

* * * * * * * *

Tobias shouted at Roxy. "Get back in your fucking office woman!" The last few months had been difficult with higher turnover than usual, but that didn't stop him from hiring and firing more frequently.

"Up yours," Roxy snapped back. It seemed everyday there was an argument between the two, and oddly enough it seemed as though they relished it. "You couldn't bring in more sales if you fired every agent here!"

"Don't test me woman. I will!" And that was usually the cue for employees to start preparing their résumés. By the end of the week an agent had been fired, but as though Roxy wouldn't be outshined she too fired an office assistant.

"I can do what you can, if not better."

"Woman, you're testing my patience!"

"Oh please, it's not like you do anything around here anyway."

"What are you talking about? I do everything!"

"And that's you're problem isn't it!"

"Why don't you delegate for once like I do."

Like a competitive game they went back and forth at the expense of their employees, making every day a new round and unnerving staff as much as it did Shannon, who after eleven months could barely step into the office without feeling like her immunity was up.

"You want to see delegation. Fine. I'll show you." He ordered an agent to sell five homes, but refused to give him any more than four. "Great. Now I have to fire him! Are you happy yet? You're just as spoiled rotten as they are."

"Look at you, driving here in your hotshot car. Mr. Big and Fancy."

"Just get back to your office."

"Don't tell me what to do."

"I'll tell you what to do, when I want, how I want! Now get back to your fucking office. I won't say it again."

"At least I have an office that I can enjoy. You let our agents run around here as if they were independent contractors or something."

"They're 10-99 employees!"

"So what? Does that mean they can do whatever they want and not follow the rules. I'm only saying what you're already thinking. You just don't want to hear it. The only reason we haven't walked away from this business already is because you're babysitting all the time." He cursed her, stormed away and took his temper out on an assistant, firing her and the agent that tried to vouch for her.

Chapter 19

Seeking New Opportunities

The interim superintendent that came after Victoria was paid $1,000 more a week than she was, and yet the Board claimed they were being more fiscally responsible.

* * * * * * * *

Shannon had had it. She gave her two week's notice, unable to stand the hostile work environment any longer. She had tried to market for Tobias and Roxy, but their counter-intuitive policies ran her efforts aground; since Tobias limited his agents and took all the rest he inadvertently stretched himself too thin and as a result negative feedback poured in.

Whatever Shannon did to remedy the situation only made matters worse. The harder she tried the more Tobias stretched himself and the negativity clashed with her efforts, making it almost superfluous.

Finally, she called it quits. She had enjoyed the challenge, but what good were her efforts if Tobias impeded them? She gave her notice, but the second she did Roxy lost her cool and exploded right in her face; all immunity was gone.

"I own you and everything you did," she shouted, grabbing the pen out of Shannon's hand. "This is all mine. Everything you did here is mine!" She went berserk and began screaming at the top of her lungs, calling Shannon disloyal and an "ungrateful employee." She even threatened to sue her if she continued in real estate at another firm, which Shannon was planning on doing; she had already been accepted by another branch. When Tobias learned of that he too went ballistic.

He called up the regional manager and demanded the other branch manager give him a written apology for being so "deceitful and unprofessional."

The man just told him to shut up. "She's still working with our brand, just at another branch location. So, why should I be upset? It's not like she's going over to our competition. She's still apart of this family brand and unless you give me a good reason I'm going to support her decision every step of the way. If she left your office, Tobias, then that's your problem. Fix your own house first before you complain about your neighbors'!"

With the regional manager's full backing, Shannon began her new job, marketing for the new branch with renewed vigor and passion as she had eleven months ago. Only this time, she was in a better place, from her new boss greeting her in the morning to more cooperative agents; she couldn't be happier. And as she started an abrupt family affair all at once put her talents in real estate to the ultimate test...